This Book Belongs to:

HANUKKAH PRAYERS

1. Baruch atah Adonai, Eloheinu melech haolam, asher kid'shanu b'mitzvotav v'tsivanu l'hadlik ner shel Hanukkah

2. Baruch atah Adonai, Eloheinu melech haolam, she-asah nisim laavoteinu v'imoteinu bayamim hahaeim baz'man hazeh

3. (**Only on first night**) Baruch atah Adonai, Eloheinu melech haolam, shehecheyanu v'kiy'manu v'higiyanu laz'man hazeh

HAPPY HANUKKAH

COLOR and COUNT

Dreidel Matching

Find the matching pairs and color them the same!

HANUKKAH WORD SEARCH

Circle words in the puzzle below

```
S P N D A S P C R
T R E R M T R M U
A E M E N O R A H
R S O I C R S C O
S E L D N A C C L
I N S E A I N A P
N T I L B E T B H
G S T U N O D E W
O I L A E E N E W
```

Menorah Maccabee presents

dreidel   star   donuts

oil   candles

HANUKKAH PATTERNS

Look at the patterns below. Cut out the images at the bottom. Paste the image that comes next in each pattern.

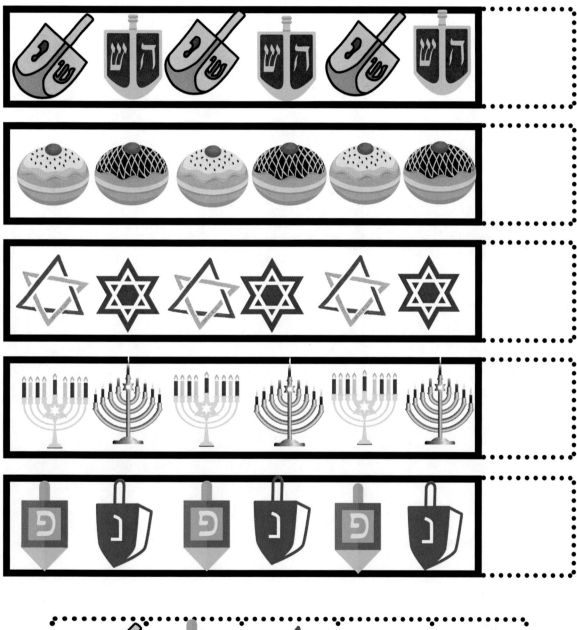

Hanukkah Alphabet Matching

Look at the picture and the upper case letter that starts the word. Match the uppercase with its lower case partner. The first one has been done for you.

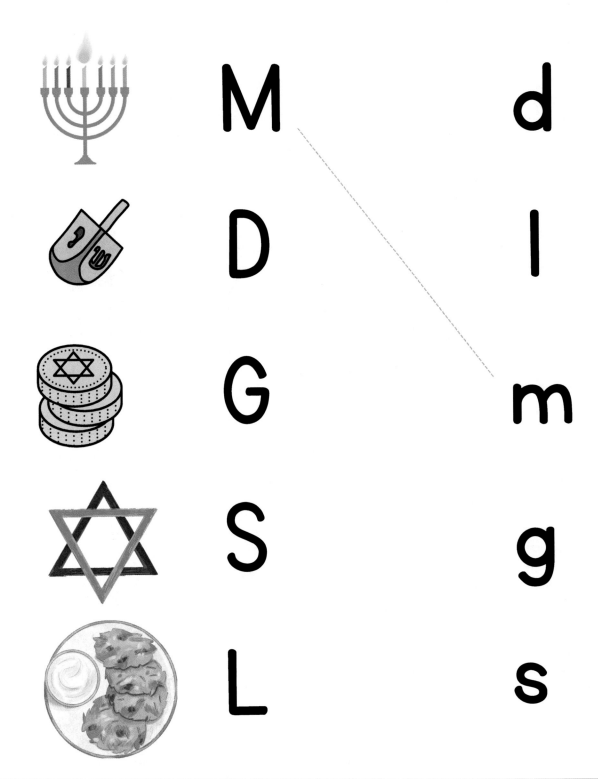

TRACE THE HANUKKAH WORDS

 Menorah

 dreidel

 gelt

 Star

 latkas

Hanukkah Sweater Design

Design and color a Hanukkah sweater below

Hanukkah Numbers and Colors

Color five dreidels red.

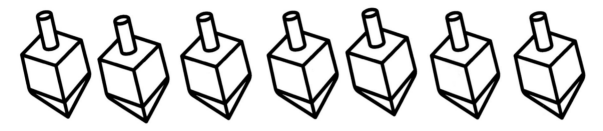

Color four dreidels green.

Color three dreidels yellow.

Color six dreidels blue.

Color two dreidels purple.

HANUKKAH GIFT COLORING

Using the colors in the key below and the shape on the tag, color the gifts below. You may use a different color for the bows.

○))purple))   ♡))yellow))

△)) red))   ☆)) blue))

HANUKKAH MATCH

Draw a line to match the number with the correct number of Hanukkah items

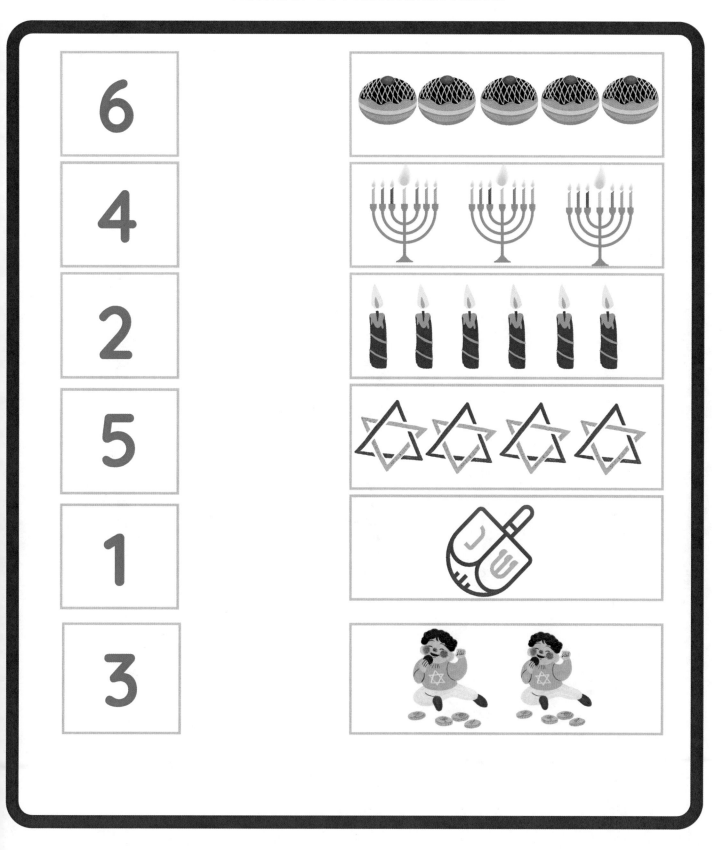

DREIDEL, DREIDEL, DREIDEL

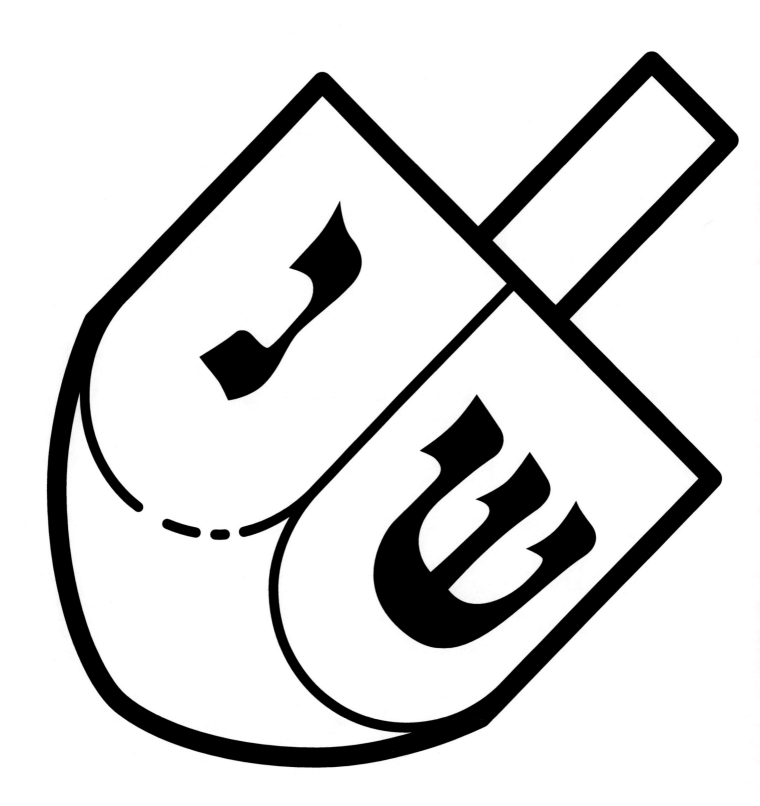

Draw a line to the matching dreidel

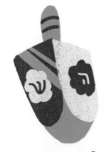

TRACE AND COLOR THE HANUKKAH PRESENTS

DECORATE THE DREIDELS

Color the numbers blue

Color the letters yellow

HANUKKAH SHADOWS

Draw a line to match the shadow of these items.

SHORT TO TALL CANDLES

Color the candles below and then cut out and organize short to tall in the space provided.

Shortest			Tallest

CONNECT THE DOTS TO MAKE THE PRESENT

COLOR THE MENORAH TO SHINE BRIGHT

COLOR THE FLAMES ORANGE

COLOR THE CANDLES BLUE

COLOR THE MENORAH YELLOW

HANUKKAH CROSSWORD

COMPLETE THE CROSSWORD PUZZLE USING THE CLUES BELOW.

WORD BOX:

CANDLE, OIL , EIGHT , DREIDEL , LATKE , MUSIC, MENORAH , SPIN

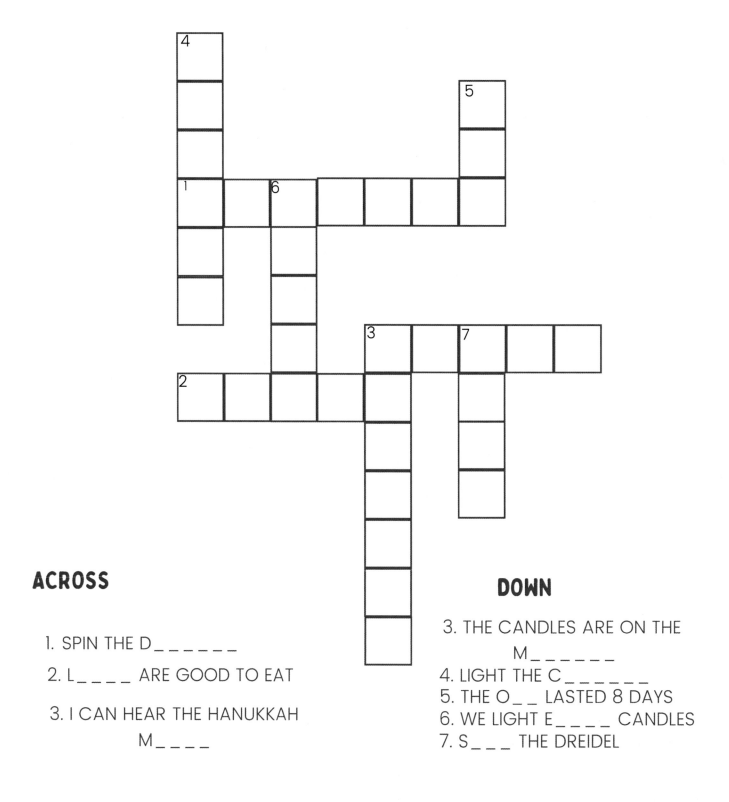

ACROSS

1. SPIN THE D _ _ _ _ _ _

2. L _ _ _ _ ARE GOOD TO EAT

3. I CAN HEAR THE HANUKKAH
   M _ _ _ _

DOWN

3. THE CANDLES ARE ON THE
   M _ _ _ _ _ _

4. LIGHT THE C _ _ _ _ _ _

5. THE O _ _ LASTED 8 DAYS

6. WE LIGHT E _ _ _ _ CANDLES

7. S _ _ _ THE DREIDEL

HANUKKAH

Write a word that starts which each letter in Hanukkah.
The first one is done for you!

H APPY _____

A _____

N _____

U _____

K _____

K _____

A _____

H _____

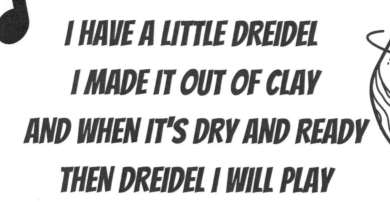

I HAVE A LITTLE DREIDEL
I MADE IT OUT OF CLAY
AND WHEN IT'S DRY AND READY
THEN DREIDEL I WILL PLAY

OH, DREIDEL, DREIDEL, DREIDEL
I MADE IT OUT OF CLAY
OH, DREIDEL,DREIDEL,DREIDEL
THEN DREIDEL I WILL PLAY

MY DREIDEL HAS A BODY
WITH LEGS SO SHORT AND THIN
WHEN IT GETS ALL TIRED,
IT DROPS AND THEN I WIN!

HANUKKAH CROSSWORD

ANSWER KEY

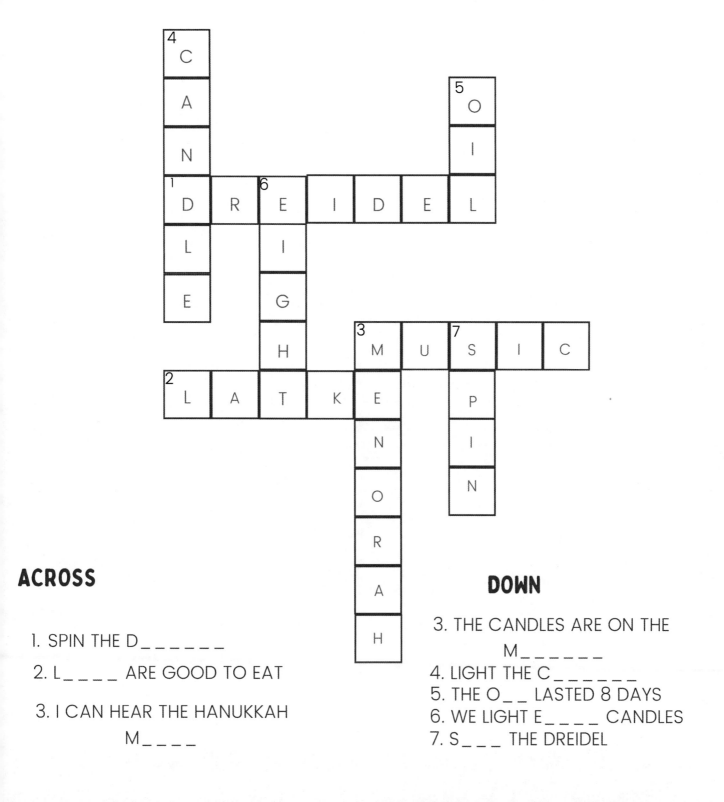

ACROSS

1. SPIN THE D _ _ _ _ _ _
2. L _ _ _ _ ARE GOOD TO EAT
3. I CAN HEAR THE HANUKKAH M _ _ _ _

DOWN

3. THE CANDLES ARE ON THE M _ _ _ _ _ _
4. LIGHT THE C _ _ _ _ _ _
5. THE O _ _ LASTED 8 DAYS
6. WE LIGHT E _ _ _ _ CANDLES
7. S _ _ _ THE DREIDEL

BY: SUSIE JACKOWITZ

Made in United States
Orlando, FL
01 December 2022

25299418R00015